Lola and I

English edition © 2015 Fitzhenry & Whiteside
Text copyright © 2012 Camelozampa

First published as "Lola e io" by Camelozampa, Main Street 8-35043 Monselice (PD), Italy
Published in Canada by Fitzhenry & Whiteside, 195 Allstate Parkway, Markham, Ontario L3R 4T8
Published in the United States by Fitzhenry & Whiteside, 311 Washington Street, Brighton, Massachusetts 02135

www.fitzhenry.ca   godwit@fitzhenry.ca

10 9 8 7 6 5 4 3 2 1

Library and Archives Canada Cataloguing in Publication

Segré, Chiara Valentina, 1982-[Lola e io. English]
Lola and I / written and translated by Chiara Valentina Segré; illustrated by Paolo Domeniconi.

Translation of: Lola e io.ISBN 978-1-55455-363-1 (bound)

        I. Domeniconi, Paolo, 1965-, illustrator II. Title. III. Title: Lola e io. English.

PZ7.1.S47Lo 2015   j853'.92   C2015-901308-9

Publisher Cataloging-in-Publication Data (U.S)

Segré, Chiara Valentina, 1982- .

Lola and I / written and translated by Chiara Valentina Segré ; illustrations by Paolo Domeniconi.

Originally published in Italian as Lola e io.

[   ] pages : color illustrations ; cm.
ISBN: 978-1-55455-363-1
1. Children with disabilities – Juvenile fiction. 2. Guide dogs – Juvenile fiction. I. Domeniconi, Paolo, 1965-.
II. Title.
[E] dc23   PZ7.1.S447 2015

Fitzhenry & Whiteside acknowledges with thanks the Canada Council for the Arts, and the Ontario Arts Council for their support of our publishing program. We acknowledge the financial support of the Government of Canada through the Canada Book Fund (CBF) for our publishing activities.

 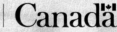

Cover and text design by Daniel Choi
Cover image by Paolo Domeniconi
Printed in China by Sheck Wah Tong Printing Press Ltd.

Lola and I

Written and translated by

Chiara Valentina Segré

Illustrations by

Paolo Domeniconi

Fitzhenry & Whiteside

Lola is my best friend. We live together in a pretty house next to a big horse chestnut tree.

Before we met, I lived happily in the countryside with my family. I was very clever at school. Lola, instead, was lonely and ill.

I loved her at first sight and decided that from that moment on, I'd take care of her. We moved into town. At first, it was not easy at all.

Lola was always sad. She would spend all day on the sofa, her eyes blank and empty. I did my best to get her to play, but Lola simply ignored me. She even refused to go out. It was really hard trying to persuade her, and when I finally did, Lola used to hug the walls.

Every sound (a policeman's whistle, a bike bell, a child's laugh) made her jump. Cars, especially, frightened her. When a horn blared or tires screeched, Lola curled up on the pavement and started to tremble. I curled up close to her until she calmed down.

Eventually, we started walking every day. We only made it to the end of the block on the first day, but we reached the park entrance the next day and the bakery at the end of the street the day after that. With each little step, Lola conquered her fear. Now, when we go strolling, Lola walks with her head up and enjoys listening to the many voices of the city.

Lola and I love each other very much, but we don't always get along.

For example, I love classical music, while Lola is crazy about rock bands. Lola can be very stubborn, so I usually go out on the balcony to get some peace.

And when it's time to cook, what a fight! Lola is crazy about fish and she wants to eat it all the time. Sure, fish is tasty and healthy, but compared to a big, juicy steak? No contest! But, as usual, Lola looks at me with her sweet eyes and I can't tell her no.

But Lola and I do have a lot of fun together. We really like shopping at our favourite clothing store. It's amazing how many clothes exist. Some are soft, velvety, or silky. Others are thick, pleated, or beaded.

Once, Lola absent-mindedly crashed into a rack of brand-new clothes. She rolled over on the floor in a heap of sleeves, skirts, silk scarves, and hats. We couldn't stop laughing, but the saleswoman didn't find it as funny.

On nice sunny days, we go to the park to enjoy the trees, the fountain, and, above all, Gigi's delicacies. Lola and I always have a table reserved under a big, red beach umbrella. With a couple of Gigi's famous cream croissants and glasses of icy lemonade, nobody is happier!

On Saturday nights, we order pizza (my favourite is pizza with hot salami, while Lola always has pizza with vegetables) and eat it on the sofa with a movie on. Thankfully, we have the same taste in movies.

Lola often falls asleep with her head on me like a pillow, and I stay still like a statue to not disturb her. It's not very comfortable, but it's so nice staying close that I don't mind.

Lola and I travel together.

In the winter, we go to the mountains to play in the snow and
go tobogganing.

In the spring, we go to the countryside and barbecue steaks, corn, and even
marshmallows. Whenever I think about it, my mouth waters. Even Lola,
who prefers fish, always eats everything we grill.

Last summer, we went to the seaside. I had never been to the beach before. The sea was a bit rough, and when I got closer to have a better look, I got caught by a sneaky wave. Salt water flew up my nose and I kept sneezing for half an hour. And Lola, that little scoundrel, laughed and ran up and down the beach.

While we were drying ourselves in the sun, a man with enormous sideburns approached us and asked if he could paint us. By sunset, we had our very own portrait. But posing for a painter is hungry work, so we stopped by the ice-cream cart and shared a cone.

That evening, we waited for the train home. With the breeze ruffling our hair, Lola told me it had been the most beautiful day of her life. And not because of the smell of the sea, or the wind on our faces, or the sun on our skin, but because I was there with her.

On Christmas Eve, five years ago, Lola lost her sight in a car crash. It had been snowing and the roads were covered in ice. Lola's car swerved off the road. She hit her head and the impact made her blind.

Two months later, Lola visited the Guide Dogs Training School.

Like I said, it was love at first sight. Even though Lola couldn't see me with her eyes, she could feel my love. She scratched me behind my ears and I wrinkled my nose on her hand. Lola chose me with no hesitation.

As we entered our new house, Lola untied my bib with the red cross and my leash. She softly whispered to me, "From now on, you will be my guide and the light of my eyes."

She named me Star.